KV-512-526

C

SAN

Please renew/return items by last date
shown. Please call the number below:

Renewals and enquiries: 0300 1234049

Textphone for hearing or
speech impaired users: 01992 555506

www.hertfordshire.gov.uk/libraries
L32

Hertfordshire

by Penny Dolan and Braden Hallett

533 343 38 1

Town Mouse lived in a grand house.
He had a nice, soft bed to sleep in
and lots of good things to eat.

One day, Town Mouse said to himself,
"I think I will go and visit my cousin,
Country Mouse."

"Welcome, Cousin!" said Country Mouse.
"You are just in time for supper."
Country Mouse gave Town Mouse
a small bowl of nuts and grain.
"Thank you," Town Mouse said,
but he did not eat very much.

4

At bedtime, Country Mouse showed
Town Mouse to his bed.

"Oh!" said Town Mouse. "Oh, dear!"

Town Mouse did not sleep very well.

Country Mouse woke his cousin up

very early the next morning.

"Come on, Cousin," he said.

"It's a bright, sunny day.

Time to get our breakfast."

The two mice worked hard gathering juicy berries, rosy apples, nuts and grains of wheat.

That evening, the two mice sat by the fireside. Country Mouse was happy. But Town Mouse was not happy.

"I do not like the country," he said.

"It is hard work, and I do not like the food."

"What do you mean, Cousin?"
asked Country Mouse.
"Come home with me tomorrow,"
Town Mouse replied. "I will show you
how good life is in town."

So off they went to Town Mouse's home. Country Mouse was amazed. They had strawberries and cream for supper and soft beds to sleep in. "You see?" said Town Mouse. "You will like living in town."

11

Next day, Country Mouse stepped into the dining room.

He saw a huge table covered with puddings and pies and delicious cakes.

"This is my sort of food, Cousin," said Town Mouse. "And we didn't even have to work to get it. Let us begin!"

Suddenly, three fierce dogs burst in. They chased the frightened mice round and round the dining room.

Town Mouse pulled Country Mouse back to the hole.

Next morning, the two mice peeped out. Everything was quiet again. "All's clear," said Town Mouse. "You can come out now."

But Country Mouse shook his head.
"Dear Cousin," he said. "In town,
you have lots of good things to eat
and a soft bed to sleep in.
But it is much safer in the country.
I am going home. Goodbye."

Country Mouse was glad to be home among the fields and hedgerows. Sometimes, as he nibbled his supper, he thought about Town Mouse in his grand house.

So Town Mouse lived in his big house in the town. Country Mouse lived in his little house in the country. And they were both very happy.

Story order

Look at these 5 pictures and captions.
Put the pictures in the right order
to retell the story.

1

The dogs chased the mice.

2

Country Mouse was glad to be home.

3

Country Mouse went to visit Town Mouse.

4

Town Mouse had to work hard.

5

Town Mouse went to visit Country Mouse.

Guide for Independent Reading

This series is designed to provide an opportunity for your child to read on their own. These notes are written for you to help your child choose a book and to read it independently.

In school, your child's teacher will often be using reading books which have been banded to support the process of learning to read. Use the book band colour your child is reading in school to help you make a good choice. *Town Mouse and Country Mouse* is a good choice for children reading at Turquoise Band in their classroom to read independently. The aim of independent reading is to read this book with ease, so that your child enjoys the story and relates it to their own experiences.

About the book
When Town Mouse visits his cousin Country Mouse, he decides that the country life is not for him. How will Country Mouse enjoy life in the town?

Before reading
Help your child to learn how to make good choices by asking: "Why did you choose this book? Why do you think you will enjoy it?" Look at the cover together and ask: "What do you think the story will be about?" Ask your child to think of what they already know about the story context. Then ask your child to read the title aloud.

Ask: "Do you think that Town Mouse and Country Mouse will like the same things?"

Remind your child that they can sound out a word in syllable chunks if they get stuck.

Decide together whether your child will read the story independently or read it aloud to you.

During reading

Remind your child of what they know and what they can do independently. If reading aloud, support your child if they hesitate or ask for help by telling the word. If reading to themselves, remind your child that they can come and ask for your help if stuck.

After reading

Support comprehension by asking your child to tell you about the story. Use the story order puzzle to encourage your child to retell the story in the right sequence, in their own words. The correct sequence can be found on the next page.

Help your child think about the messages in the book that go beyond the story and ask: "Why do you think Town Mouse didn't like life in the country? Why do you think Country Mouse didn't like life in the town?" Give your child a chance to respond to the story: "Do you think there is a lesson in this story? What do you think it is?"

Extending learning

Help your child understand the story structure by using the same sentence patterning and adding different elements. "Let's make up a new story about Town Mouse and Country Mouse. Where might they visit this time and will they both like it? How about a theatre or a rainforest?"

In the classroom, your child's teacher may be teaching use of punctuation marks. Ask your child to identify some question marks and exclamation marks in the story and then ask them to practise reading each of the whole sentences with appropriate expression.

Franklin Watts
First published in Great Britain in 2021
by The Watts Publishing Group

Series Editors: Jackie Hamley and Melanie Palmer
Series Advisors: Dr Sue Bodman and Glen Franklin
Series Designers: Peter Scoulding and Cathryn Gilbert

A CIP catalogue record for this book is
available from the British Library.

ISBN 978 1 4451 7416 7 (hbk)
ISBN 978 1 4451 7417 4 (pbk)
ISBN 978 1 4451 7538 6 (library ebook)
ISBN 978 1 4451 8147 9 (ebook)

Printed in China

Franklin Watts
An imprint of
Hachette Children's Group
Part of The Watts Publishing Group
Carmelite House
50 Victoria Embankment
London EC4Y 0DZ

An Hachette UK Company
www.hachette.co.uk

www.franklinwatts.co.uk

FSC
www.fsc.org
MIX
Paper from
responsible sources
FSC® C104740

Answer to Story order: 5, 4, 3, 1, 2